CONTENTS

6   STORY: Once upon a time ...

8   Meet the Characters:
In a world with Shrek

10   STORY: Happy Birthday

12   It's a Deal!

13   Piles of Presents!

14   Meet the Characters:
In a world without Shrek

16   STORY: A world that made sense

18   Which Witch Has Shrek?

21   How Many Witches?

22   Meet the Characters:
In a world with Shrek

23   Meet the Characters:
In a world without Shrek

24   What's in a Name?

25   Come Fly with Me

26   STORY: Looking for love/
Shrek's Daydream

30   Colouring-in Pages

32   Ogling Ogres

34   Bits and Pieces

35   Creamed Out

36   STORY: At Rumpel's palace

41   Jokes

42   Dance Partner

43   Codebreaker

44   STORY: The search for Shrek

50   Who's Who?

51   Dot-to-Dot

52   STORY: The final countdown

58   Home Sweet Home

59   Shrek Trivia

60   Activity Answers

SHREK FOREVER AFTER: ANNUAL 2011 • A BANTAM BOOK 978 0 553 82232 8 • Published in Great Britain by Bantam, an imprint of Random House Children's Books • A Random House Group Company • This edition published 2010
1 2 3 4 5 6 7 8 9 10

Shrek Forever After ™ & © 2010 DreamWorks Animation L.L.C. • Shrek is a registered trademark of DreamWorks Animation L.L.C. • All rights reserved • Bantam Books are published by Random House Children's Books. • 61–63 Uxbridge Road, London W5 5SA
www.rbooks.co.uk • www.kidsatrandomhouse.co.uk

Addresses for companies within The Random House Group Limited can be found at: www.randomhouse.co.uk/offices.htm
THE RANDOM HOUSE GROUP Limited Reg. No. 954009
A CIP catalogue record for this book is available from the British Library • Printed in the UK by Butler Tanner and Dennis

Once upon a time...

On a dark and stormy night, a royal carriage pulled up outside a shabby-looking trailer, its sign read: "Magical Contracts". Inside, King Harold and Queen Lilian had given up hope that a brave knight would rescue their beautiful daughter and release her from the terrible curse that turned her into a hideous ogre at night. Full of despair, they had decided to take desperate measures; they had come to see . . .

"Rumpelstiltskin!" the little man cried as he jumped off his chair and kissed the queen's hand. Placing a contract on the desk, he explained that everything was in order. With just a signature from King Harold, Rumpelstiltskin would lift his daughter's curse. All he asked in return was for King Harold to sign over control of Far Far Away to him. After a short moment of doubt, King Harold placed his hand on the contract and went to sign it.

"Nothing is worth more to us than our daughter," he said.

Rumpelstiltskin watched anxiously as the king moved to sign when the door burst open!

"Your Highness! The princess! She's been saved!" a royal messenger cried.

Luckily for all the people of Far Far Away, Shrek saved Princess Fiona. He turned out to be her One True Love. They married, had three ogre babies, Fergus, Farkle and Felicia, and they all lived happily ever after! Meanwhile, Rumpel's dreams were dashed and he wished that Shrek had never been born . . .

Shrek lived a life he had never dreamed possible. His days were filled changing smelly nappies, feeding babies and cleaning the outhouse. Tour buses full of people eager to see a loveable lug of an ogre drove past his house every day. Shrek loved being a dad and a husband but sometimes he really missed being the plain old, scary ogre he used to be.

In a world with Shrek . . .

SHREK

Shrek, the ogre with a heart of gold, had it all. A happy home, great friends, the perfect loving wife and three super-stinky ogre babies, Fergus, Farkle and Felicia. But a perfectly happy life didn't always make him perfectly happy. When Shrek remembered his old life without fame, stinky nappies and responsibilities, he began to wonder whether his "happily ever after" was really all it was cracked up to be. And as he unclogged the outhouse for the umpteenth time, he started to yearn for the freedom and fun he once had. What would life be like if he could go back to being a real ogre just for one little day . . .

FIONA

Fiona was the happiest ogre in all of Far Far Away! She was living her "happily ever after" and loved it! What more could she have asked for? A loving husband, three adorable babies and the most swamp-tastic home in the world. Sure, it was tough living in the limelight as the wife of the kingdom's most-loved ogre. And of course it was hard work being a full-time mum, spending her days feeding, bathing and nappy-changing three baby ogres, but would she change a thing? No way! No task was too tough for this feisty princess.

OGRE BABIES

Fergus, Farkle and Felicia were the rotten apples of their proud parents' eyes! They burped like their mum and made big, grown-up ogre stinks, just like their dad. And with Donkey, Dragon and their baby dronkeys around, every day was just one big playdate.

PUSS IN BOOTS

By day, Puss In Boots was still a swash-buckling, sword-wielding, courageous hero. By night, he kicked back and relaxed with the three best friends a feline could have wished for. Yes, this was the cat who had got the cream and there wasn't a night that went by when he wasn't strumming his guitar and regaling his friends with tall tales of how Shrek and Fiona met, fell in love and lived happily ever after.

DONKEY

Donkey was just so happy he could break into song! And he did … frequently. Nothing made this four-legged chatterbox happier and more full of beans than when he was hanging out with his hot wife, their dronkey babies and Shrek's happy family.

Happy Birthday

It was the ogre babies' first birthday and Shrek and Fiona were having a party at the Candy Apple. But things didn't get off to a good start. The same villagers who used to be scared of Shrek now asked for his autograph!

"Oh man, you used to be so fierce!" they cried. "When you were a real ogre."

Shrek didn't feel like singing, or giving a big ogre roar for Butter Pants when he asked for one. The cake was awful and then Donkey licked it! While Butter Pants carried on pestering him for a roar, Fiona rushed to find the candles Shrek had forgotten. But as soon as his back was turned, the Three Little Pigs ate the cake! The babies started

crying. Butter Pants still wanted a roar and the babies just cried even louder.

"Do the roar! Do the roar! Do the roar!" the guests chanted.

"We need the cake. The cake!" cried Fiona.

"Wah! Wah! Wah!" screamed the babies.

"ROOOOOOAAAAAARRRRRRRRRRR!!!!" Shrek just couldn't take any more.

"Woo-hoo!" yelled the crowd.

Frustrated, Shrek stormed outside and Fiona followed. Neither of them noticed Rumpelstiltskin hiding in the garbage behind the Candy Apple.

"I used to be an ogre!" cried Shrek. "Now I'm just a jolly green joke. All I want is for things to go back to the way they used to be. When I could do what I wanted, when I wanted. Back when the world made sense."

Fiona was hurt. "Shrek, you have everything," she said as she turned to go back to the party. "Why is it that the only person who can't see that is you."

As Shrek stormed off, Rumpel peered out from behind the rubbish bins. He had a plan . . .

On his way home, Shrek was tricked into accepting a lift from Rumpelstiltskin. Over a few eyeballtinis in Rumpel's trailer, Shrek was soon getting all his troubles off his chest.

"Sometimes I wish I had just one day to feel like a real ogre again," he moaned.

"Well, to make the magic work," explained Rumpel, "you've got to give a day to get a day. That's all." And Shrek needn't worry about his family, he continued. "No one will ever know you're gone!"

"So, what day would I have to give up?" asked Shrek.

"Any day," replied Rumpel. Maybe one from Shrek's childhood, one he doesn't even remember.

"There's nothing wrong with wanting a little time for myself," reasoned Shrek. "I'm still my own ogre! I've never had to ask anyone's permission before," he cried, signing the contract.

"Have a nice day!" sneered Rumpel. Suddenly everything went black . . .

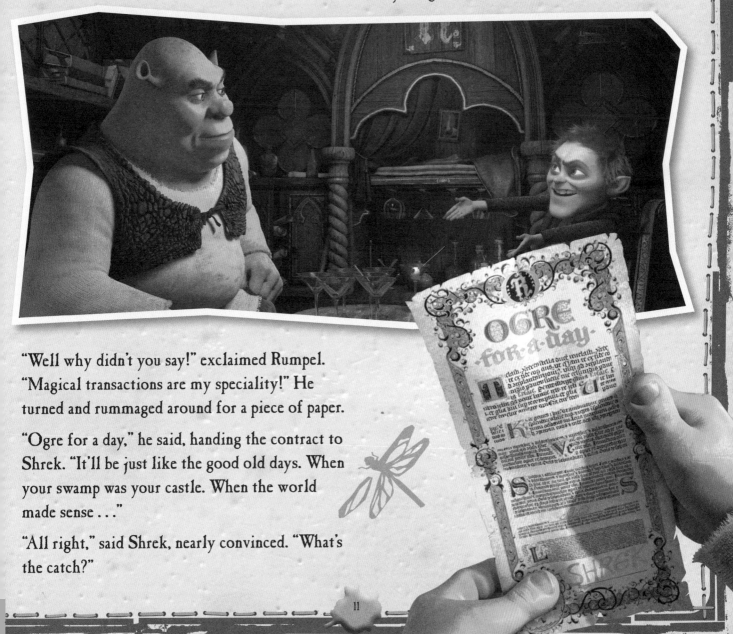

"Well why didn't you say!" exclaimed Rumpel. "Magical transactions are my speciality!" He turned and rummaged around for a piece of paper.

"Ogre for a day," he said, handing the contract to Shrek. "It'll be just like the good old days. When your swamp was your castle. When the world made sense . . ."

"All right," said Shrek, nearly convinced. "What's the catch?"

IT'S A DEAL!

Make your very own Rumpelstiltskin contract.
Just fill in the spaces to make a foolproof contract
to get whatever you want!

This contract officially
declares that I,

....

am allowed for the period
of one whole day to

....

....

and nobody else is allowed to

....

....

or

....

....

and I'm allowed to stay up till

....

and my room can be as

....

as I like it.

Signed

....

Countersigned

Rumpelstiltskin

PILES OF PRESENTS!

There's been a muddle at Fergus, Farkle and Felicia's birthday party – the babies have got lost in all their presents. Look carefully at the picture below and see if you can spot the three ogre babies and count how many of each present there are.

Answers on page 61

In a world WITHOUT Shrek . . .

SHREK

What Shrek didn't realize when he signed Rumpel's contract was that the day he exchanged for his ogre day was the day he was born. That meant he never existed, and in a world without Shrek, everything was very different. With no one to rescue Princess Fiona, King Harold signed over control of the kingdom to Rumpelstiltskin. And Rumpel was a pretty nasty ruler. The inhabitants of Far Far Away lived in fear of his cadre of witches who terrorized the land and rounded up ogres to work in Rumpel's chain gangs.

FIONA

In a world without Shrek, Princess Fiona sat in her tall tower waiting to be rescued. But she didn't wait for long. When she realized that no knight in shining armour was coming for her, she took matters into her own hands – the feisty princess decided to rescue herself! Under Rumpel's rule all ogres were considered dangerous so Fiona was forced to live in the forest with her outlaw band of ogres who had the same goal: they wanted to rid Far Far Away of Rumpel, the curly-toed weirdo!

14

OGRE BABIES

Sadly, in a world where Shrek and Fiona had never met, it was impossible for Fergus, Farkle and Felicia to have been born.

PUSS IN BOOTS

Puss was no longer the fearsome assassin he once was. Sent by Rumpel to track Fiona, he was won over by her charm. As her favourite and most-pampered pet, he had grown fat and tubby from living the good life and had become too slow and lazy to fight any battles. He was her trusted confidant and the only creature to know her dreadful secret: that the mighty ogre warrior Fiona turned into a human princess during the day!

DONKEY

Without a friend in the world, poor Donkey had become an unkempt beast of burden. His coat was shaggy and his job was to pull the witches' prison carriage. He kept his spirits up by breaking into song, but the witches whipped him till he sang a song that they liked!

A world that made sense

A confused Shrek looked at the contract in his hand. Suddenly, he heard the sound of the Star Tours Chariot approaching.

"And as we head over the river and through the woods, we come across . . ." chattered the tour guide as the chariot rolled along.

"OGRE!" screamed one of the tour party as the carriage crashed into a tree.

The tourists ran away in fright as Shrek looked gleefully at the contract in his hand. He was stunned. It had really worked.

16

That morning, Shrek had great fun. Sauntering towards a nearby village, he frightened the group of people standing at the gates. Then he scared a bunch of kids watching a puppet show. Next he terrorized a wedding party. After he'd scared everyone in town he was left alone in a deep and gloopy mud bath. Ogre bliss.

After such a busy morning Shrek took a walk through the woods and admired all the OGRES WANTED posters.

"Sure is great to be wanted again!" he laughed. But then, one particular poster caught his eye. The picture was of a female ogre with red hair that looked just like . . .

"Fiona?" he whispered. A thought struck him. If Fiona was a wanted ogre, then she had to be in danger! He ran off at top speed towards his home.

Back at the swamp everything was deserted.

"My home . . ." he cried, flinging himself at the tree stump that should have been his house. "Fiona! Are you in there?!" he yelled, breaking through the wall. But the only living thing inside was a rat. His family was nowhere to be seen.

"All right, Rumpel," he bellowed to the empty swamp. "This wasn't part of the deal."

The surrounding swamp remained silent.

The silence was broken by a '*zoom-zoom*' noise and flashes of orange light overhead. Screeches of "OGRE!!!" swiftly followed. Looking up, Shrek saw a squadron of cackling witches above.

"What are you doing in my swamp?!" he shouted as one witch swooped towards him. Shrek stepped out of the way and grabbed her broom, which sent the witch hurtling into a tree.

"A troublemaker," Merciel sneered, and grabbed an apple from her cauldron. She bit the tip off and hurled it at Shrek.

In an instant, he was choking on the purple fumes from the apple bomb. It wasn't long before skull handcuffs were biting into his arm and legs and the witches lifted him up into the air.

"You witches are making a big mistake," he roared, putting up a struggle. "I know my rights."

"You have the right to shut your mouth!" snapped Giovanna as she tossed a pumpkin bomb towards Shrek. It exploded in a puff of black smoke and knocked him out.

WHICH WITCH HAS SHREK?

Can you work out which witch has shackled Shrek?

A   B   C

Answer ☐

Answers on page 61

Shrek awoke to hear a very familiar voice.

"Donkey, stop singing, will you?" he said groggily as he sat up and banged his head on the roof of his cage. Donkey was pulling the carriage Shrek was chained in, singing as he went.

"Donkey, where am I?" he cried as a witch's whip cracked down on Donkey's back and Donkey quickly changed song.

"Look, ogre, I think you must have confused me with some other talking donkey. I've never seen you before in my life."

"It's me, Shrek!" said Shrek, growing increasingly puzzled. "Your best friend."

Donkey was shocked. The idea of a donkey and an ogre being friends was the most ridiculous thing he'd ever heard!

"Can you at least tell me where they're taking me?" Shrek asked.

"To Rumpelstiltskin," Donkey replied.

Shrek looked around. The letters of the Far Far Away sign lay in ruins and in the distance sat a giant Fabergé-egg palace where King Harold and Queen Lilian's castle once stood.

As the carriage rolled through the gates to Rumpel's palace, Shrek saw crowds of jeering peasants gathered around a fight ring. Standing in the middle was Gingy, now a hardened gladiator cookie, who was slicing the heads off a herd of animal crackers as onlookers placed bets on who would win the fight.

Once inside the palace walls Shrek spied a chain gang of enslaved ogres doing hard labour. He looked on with sadness and confusion.

As Shrek was hauled from his cage he bent down to Donkey.

"Don't worry, Donkey," he whispered as the witches pulled him off. "I'll get our life back."

"Yeah, right. Put a little mustard on mine, Captain Crazy," replied Donkey as the witches dragged Shrek through the doors to the throne room.

Shrek was led to Rumpelstiltskin, who was surrounded by partying witches.

"Ladies," Rumpel gloated. 'This is the guy who made all this possible. Tell me, how are you enjoying your day?"

"All right, Rumpel, what's going on? What have you done?" retorted Shrek.

"Oh no, Shrek, it's not what I've done. It's what *you've* done." Rumpel explained that with no Shrek to rescue their daughter, King Harold and Queen Lilian signed Far Far Away over to him to end Fiona's curse.

"But I ended Fiona's curse," cried Shrek.

"How could you when you never existed?" said Rumpel smugly.

Shrek was really confused. So Rumpel spelled it out for him. He reminded Shrek that he gave Rumpel a day from his childhood, when he was a teeny tiny baby.

Shrek finally realized what he'd done. "You took the day I was born!?"

"No, Shrek." Rumpel smiled with glee. "You gave it to me. Since you were never born, once this day comes to an end . . . so will you."

"Where's Fiona? Where's my family?" Now Shrek was really angry.

"Ha. Silly little ogre, you don't get it, do you? You see, you never met Fiona. Your kids don't exist," Rumpel gloated.

This was too much for Shrek to bear. He broke free of his chains, grabbed a broom from a passing witch, climbed on board and zoomed off through the palace. Several witches gave chase but Shrek outwitted them and grabbed Donkey.

Then something shiny caught Shrek's eye. He grabbed hold of the giant disco ball which hung from the ceiling and smashed through the glass roof, pulling the disco ball behind them to block their exit and any witches who were following.

"Not my pretty ball!" shrieked Rumpel as it wobbled, fell to the floor and smashed into a thousand pieces.

Rumpel was beside himself with rage. He looked on and screeched, "Wolfie! My angry wig."

HOW MANY WITCHES?

How many wicked witches can you spot flying after Shrek?

Miles away, Shrek and Donkey were still on their broomstick.

"I've been kidnapped!" cried Donkey as they crash-landed. He ran off but Shrek tackled him to the ground.

"Please, please eat my face last and send my hooves to my mama!" Donkey yelped.

After trying hard to persuade Donkey to be his friend, Shrek finally gave up. Defeated, he let him run away. He sat on a tree stump and pulled Felicia's favourite toy, Sir Squeakles, out of his pocket. A sad, solitary tear rolled down his face.

"I've never seen an ogre cry," said a familiar voice. Donkey was back! Shrek told him about the contract Rumpel had conned him into signing.

"You should never sign a contract with Rumpelstiltskin," said Donkey, but then he mentioned the exit clause. With some expert origami, Donkey neatly folded the paper so that it spelled out:

"Try Lou's Bliss!"

"Give me that," Shrek cried. He re-folded the contract to reveal the words: "True Love's Kiss". He was suddenly full of hope. "If Fiona and I share True Love's Kiss, I will get my life back!"

Now all Shrek and Donkey had to do was find Fiona.

Answers on page 61

Answer

In a world with Shrek

RUMPELSTILTSKIN

The curly-toed weirdo has certainly fallen on hard times. Living in his caravan in the Crone's Nest Carriage Park, filled with witches and warlocks of less than reputable character, Rumpel and his beloved goose, Fifi, manage to get by. The kingdom of Far Far Away was a happy and peaceful place and no one needed his magical contracts! No one, that is, until he bumps into Shrek . . .

WITCHES

The witches of Far Far Away were a bunch of outcasts. Living on the outskirts of the kingdom in a rundown trailer park, they lived by their own rules, and scared away any trespassers or unwanted visitors.

PINOCCHIO

The wooden boy who wanted to be real had a pretty happy and contented life working in the village bookstore. Not even the temptation of one of Rumpel's magical contracts would persuade him to change.

THE THREE LITTLE PIGS

These guys knew how to party! Always hungry, they knew the best places to hang out to get their trotters on some sweet and tasty treats, which is why they could be found hard at work in the Candy Apple!

GINGY

Gingy was the most contented gingerbread man in the kingdom. Working at the Candy Apple and living with the Muffin Man was brilliant! Where else could a biscuit get iced chaps whenever he wanted?

THE BIG BAD WOLF

Life was pretty easy for the Big Bad Wolf. He could always find a spare bed to crash in!

In a world WITHOUT Shrek

RUMPEL

That's King Rumpel to anyone who's asking! In a world without Shrek, Rumpel was king of Far Far Away, and with his cadre of wicked witches he ruled the land with a tiny but iron fist. He lived the life of luxury, a far-flung cry from his pokey trailer. His palace was immense, complete with disco room and shiny disco ball!

WITCHES

Acting as Rumpel's henchmen, these witches had a field day exercising their passion for being mean and nasty. If anyone crossed Rumpel they'd better watch out. These crafty ladies, would be hot on their tails ready to pumpkin-bomb them to oblivion!

PINOCCHIO

Life took a bad turn for Pinocchio. He was ridiculed and unwanted, so yet again his only hope and desire was to become a real boy, and signing one of Rumpel's contracts was the only way he would be able to do it!

GINGY

Life was pretty hard for Gingy in a world without Shrek. He had to shelve his dreams of being a cowboy and was forced to make his living as a gingerbread gladiator. Entering the arena day after day to fight a menagerie of animal crackers was very undignified!

THE THREE LITTLE PIGS

The Three Little Pigs were working for Rumpel, taking care of Fifi and serving food day in and day out. And what sort of food did Rumpel and his goose Fifi eat? Why, only pork! Poor Little Pigs.

THE BIG BAD WOLF

At Rumpelstiltskin's beck and call was the Big Bad Wolf. He was wig-maker extraordinaire because Rumpel sure did love his wigs! He had one for every occasion, but when Shrek started to make trouble, it was the angry wig that got used the most!

WHAT'S IN A NAME?

Can you find all the characters' names
in the wordsearch below?

Shrek   Dragon   Puss In Boots

Donkey   Farkle   Felicia

Gingy

Fiona   Rumpelstiltskin

Wolfie   Fergus   Pinocchio

P	A	D	D	E	I	F	L	O	W	Q	U	I	T	P
R	I	N	A	P	O	Y	Y	B	S	A	T	U	L	U
Q	A	N	O	I	F	U	A	S	M	N	B	B	O	S
X	P	V	O	Y	B	G	T	Z	F	E	R	G	U	S
C	I	O	B	C	Y	N	U	T	A	U	A	I	O	I
V	W	O	F	E	C	S	R	P	R	X	U	N	F	N
W	M	B	K	P	S	H	R	E	K	O	I	G	A	B
P	R	N	C	E	S	F	I	E	L	C	I	Y	R	O
A	O	D	R	G	O	N	F	O	E	I	O	N	G	O
D	F	R	G	Z	W	R	E	K	R	A	P	O	B	T
R	X	A	I	C	I	L	E	F	R	P	A	R	D	S
A	P	U	Q	Z	X	T	R	E	E	Y	V	D	S	A
G	U	S	S	D	K	N	O	Y	A	C	V	B	M	W
O	M	C	S	S	E	O	I	Y	N	M	C	V	S	A
N	I	K	S	T	L	I	T	S	L	E	P	M	U	R

Answers on page 61

24

COME FLY WITH ME

Shrek and Donkey have escaped Rumpel's castle on a stolen broom.
Using the map co-ordinates below, draw a path on the map
that will help them get to safety.

MAP CO-ORDINATES: 3W, 1S, 2SW, 1S, 1E, 1S, 4E, 1S, 2SE, 1S, 2E

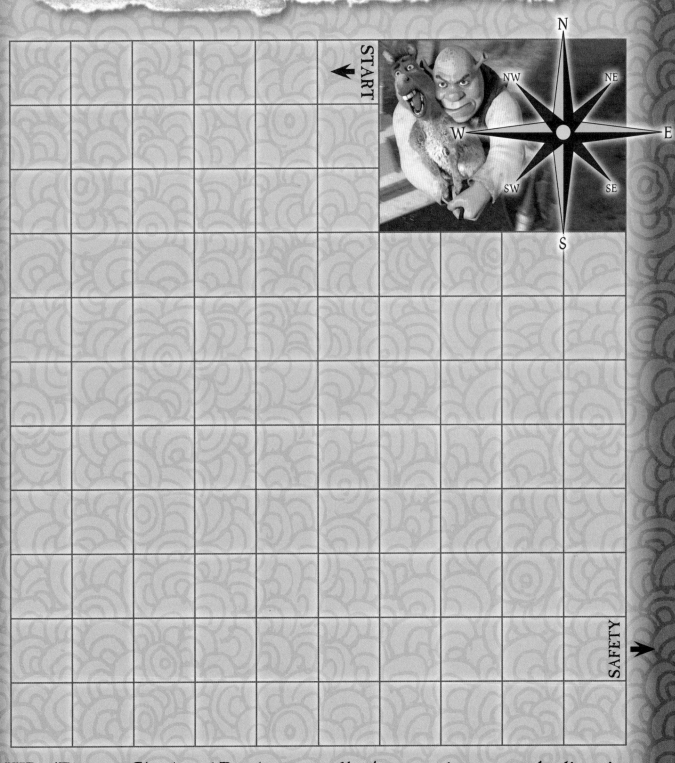

TIP: 4E means Shrek and Donkey must fly 4 squares in an easterly direction;
2S means they must fly 2 squares in a southerly direction.

Answers on page 61

Looking for love

Shrek rushed to the dragon's keep but all he found was an empty room, Fiona's crown and the handkerchief she once gave to Shrek for rescuing her. He sadly picked it up and left the empty tower.

Back at the palace, Rumpel was mad! If Shrek kissed Fiona before sunrise then Rumpel's reign would be over!

"Does anyone care to tell me what it's going to take to get this ogre?" said a peeved Rumpel, addressing his witches.

"A professional bounty hunter?" suggested one.

"NO!!" shouted Rumpel as he flung a glass of water over her and she melted away.

But then he changed his mind . . . maybe a bounty hunter was exactly what he needed. And Rumpel knew the perfect person.

SHREK'S DAYDREAM

Can you rearrange the letters below to work out what Shrek's daydreaming about?

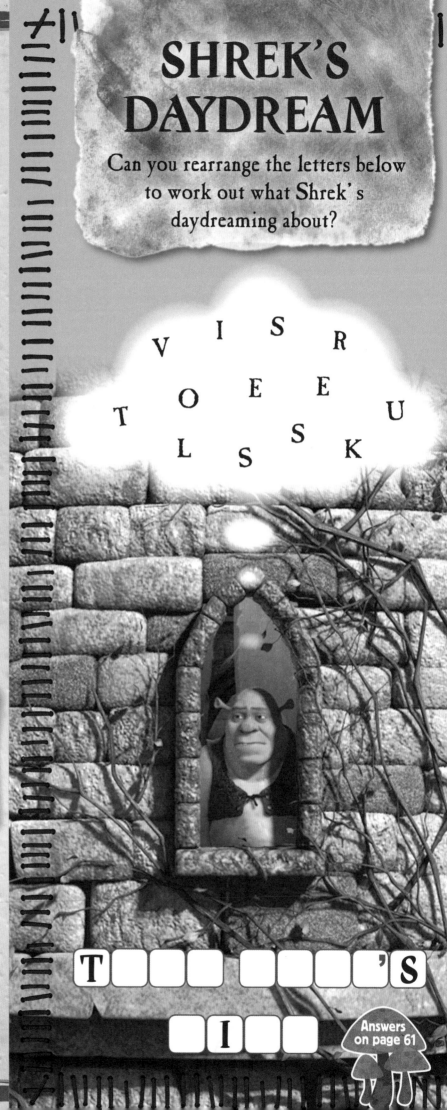

V I S R
T O E E U
L S S K

T ☐ ☐ ☐ ☐ E K ☐ ☐ 'S

☐ I ☐ ☐

Answers on page 61

Outside the tower, Shrek looked forlornly at Fiona's hankie before he shoved it under Donkey's nose. Maybe Donkey could track down Fiona using its scent!

"Do I look like a bloodhound to you?!" cried Donkey, offended. "In case you haven't noticed, I'm a donkey, not a dog. If I was a dog, they'd call me 'Dog', not 'Donkey'. And another thing—" Donkey stopped to sniff the ground. "Wait a minute. I think I've got something."

"Fiona?" asked Shrek hopefully.

But Donkey wasn't listening. He was already charging off through the brush.

The pair came to a clearing. Sitting suspiciously on a tree stump was a pile of hot waffles.

"Donkey! Don't eat that!" Shrek cried. But it was too late. As donkey licked the waffle the plate disappeared and a swinging log knocked him into a hole. Shrek looked down just in time to see a rope loop around Donkey's tail and pull him off. Shrek jumped after him and followed the sound of Donkey's voice till he came to an opening through which he could see ... a whole camp full of ogres!

"Hey, it's a new guy!" Private Jammy yelled, pointing at Shrek.

The ogre soldiers immediately start measuring Shrek up for some armour. Once he had been kitted out with full battle armour it was time for training.

"Welcome to the resistance," Brogan said as he approached Shrek.

"We fight for freedom, and ogres everywhere!" he cried, holding his nose and blowing hard. A loud 'toot toot a toot' sound came from his ears!

"TOOT TOOT A TOOT!" replied all the other ogres.

Shrek was marvelling at this new discovery when he heard an unmistakable voice calling for help. Following the sound he found Donkey tied to a spit. Two huge ogres stood near by.

"I'll take him," Shrek said bravely. "This order's to go."

Things started to get heated when Brogan arrived but then ...

"Enough!" shouted Fiona, standing in full battle gear. "Save your fight for Rumpelstiltskin."

Shrek rushed towards the leader of the ogres, but when he reached her, his face was met with ... her foot! She didn't even recognize him.

"Ha! Owned!" laughed a soldier.

Shrek ran after Fiona and tried to explain that they were married.

"Whoa, I guess I must have hit him harder than I thought," Fiona said before she stalked off towards the war room. Shrek realized that making her fall in love with him was going to be tough work.

Inside a hollow tree in the ogre camp, Fiona and her most-trusted aides looked intently at a map of Far Far Away. Fiona told the ogres that Rumpelstiltskin was rumoured to be heading tonight's patrol himself. The plan was to ambush the patrol.

Once inside, a shocking sight met Shrek's eyes. Puss In Boots was there ... but he was not his usual slim-line self! A fat cat slid from his carpeted condo.

"Feed me, if you dare," he challenged Shrek.

"Spread the word," Fiona ordered. "We move out as soon as Rumpel leaves the palace."

Whilst listening in to the plan, Shrek had been planning his own ambush – on Fiona. If he could make Fiona fall in love with him once, then he could do it again. He grabbed a passing frog, blew it up into a balloon and headed towards Fiona's tent.

Shrek couldn't believe what he was seeing. "Puss? Where's your hat? Where's your belt? Your wee little boots?"

Puss told Shrek he was in retirement now and very happy. He had all the cream he could drink and all the mice he could catch. But when a cheeky mouse scurried up and drank out of Puss's bowl, he was way too fat and lazy to chase him away. Shrek was appalled at what had happened to Puss.

He promised to fix it all,
if Puss would just help
him kiss Fiona.

Just then, Fiona walked in.

"Can I help you with
something?" she asked.

Shrek revealed his gift
basket and frog balloon.
"A little something to ease
the tension." Inside, there
was a heart-shaped box
of slugs, a skunk-scented
candle and a book of hand-
drawn coupons.

"Let's see . . ." Shrek said.
"Good for one free foot
massage. A mud facial.
Oh, and here's one. Good
for one free kiss. Let's cash
that now." Shrek leaned
forward and puckered up.

Fiona was appalled. How
could he disturb her whilst
she was trying to run a
revolution! She twisted
Shrek's arm behind his
back and marched him out
of the tent.

COLOUR THIS

Warrior Fiona has traded her dresses for battle gear.
Take a look at the picture and copy the colours,
or give her outfit your own twist.

COLOUR THIS

Puss In Boots is not the cat he used to be, but he's happy as Fiona's much-loved pet.

Using the picture below, can you copy the colours to fill in this picture?

OGLING OGRES

Take a close look at these two pictures of the ogre army.
Can you spot the 10 differences between each picture?

Answers on page 61

BITS AND PIECES

Can you work out which of these missing pieces
will complete the picture below?

Answers on page 61

Answer ☐ ☐ ☐

CREAMED OUT

Fat Puss is feeling peckish but he's too lazy
to get the cream by himself. Can you guide him
through the maze to his dinner?

Answers on page 61

At Rumpel's palace . . .

Rumpelstiltskin's beloved pet goose, Fifi, was getting the royal treatment from Rumpel's loyal servants.

"Don't forget to floss her!" Rumpel shouted out to one of the Three Pigs, who was attempting to clean Fifi's teeth without getting his eye pecked out!

"And be careful with her nails!" he warned another Pig, who was trying to clip her claws without getting scratched.

"And don't miss under her wings!" he screamed at the last poor Pig as he desperately tried to clean her white feathers.

"Daddy thinks you look real nice, Fifi," Rumpel said to his pet.

"All right, piggies, be gone!" The Three Pigs spritzed Fifi with perfume, and ran out of the room just as Griselda, one of Rumpel's witches, announced the arrival of a guest.

"Mr Stiltskin! He's here!" she called.

A mysterious figure entered the palace, riding on a huge wave of rats.

"Pied Piper. How was your journey?" asked Rumpel. The Pied Piper tooted his flute in musical response.

Griselda laughed at Rumpel's choice of a bounty hunter. "What's he going to do?" she asked. "Flute those ogres a lullaby?"

As the witches chuckled, the Pied Piper played his flute and the witches suddenly started to break-dance, They were completely out of control!

"Looks like it's time to pay the piper," smiled Rumpel smugly.

Back at the ogre camp, Shrek was determined to win Fiona's affection – so he tried another tactic.

Fiona was practising her sparring skills, Shrek approached with an axe.

"Hello! Don't mind me," he said casually.

"What are you doing?" asked Fiona.

"What does it look like? I'm getting ready for ambush action. Oh yeah, I always like to quad my lutes and do some scrunches before an operational op." Shrek pointed to a funny-looking weapon. "This one taken?"

"We use that to clean the toilets," answered an unimpressed Fiona.

"Ah." Shrek picked up another weapon.

"And we use that one to clean the thing we clean the toilets with," said Fiona.

This was not going well! Shrek picked up a third weapon and this time he managed to loft it dead-centre into a witch dummy – by a total fluke! He let out a confident laugh.

"Hey, Scott?" said Fiona.

"It's, um, Shrek, actually."

"I know this is all a big joke to you, but we've lost everything because of Rumpelstiltskin," explained Fiona.

"I know . . . So did I," answered Shrek sincerely.

"Well, you're going to get yourself killed at the ambush tonight," she warned him.

"I'll be fine. I think I can take care of myself," he replied.

Fiona threw a shield into Shrek's arms and they began sparring. They used every weapon they could find, and soon found themselves in hand-to-hand combat. Finally, they grabbed each other face-to-face and looked into each other's eyes. For a brief moment, Shrek saw the Fiona he once shared a life with . . .

"OK, good. It seems like you can handle yourself," said Fiona as she pulled away.

"Fiona—" Shrek implored.

"Now go get ready for the mission," she commanded.

"I will, but, Fiona, if I—"

"That's an order," Fiona shouted as she walked off alone.

That night, the ogres prepared for their mission. Fiona went ahead to give the signal for the troops to attack. From the lookout spot, she waited for Rumpel's carriage to come into sight.

"It's quite a view from up here," said Shrek, appearing behind her.

"What are you doing? Get back in position!" she ordered.

"You need to know once and for all," Shrek replied.

"You're going to ruin everything!" answered Fiona.

"Ruin everything? Actually, I'm going to fix everything. The ogres, Rumpel, your curse," Shrek said.

"How do you know about my curse?" asked Fiona. She was so stunned she failed to notice Rumpel's carriage passing by her.

"Where's Fiona's signal?" Brogan asked as the camouflaged ogres lay in wait. They watched Rumpel's carriage roll past, surrounded by guard witches.

"He's going to get away," said Cookie.

"No, he's not," reassured Brogan as he signalled

for the ogres to attack. The witches scattered and the ogres tore the carriage apart, but Rumpel was nowhere to be found.

A tooting noise came from behind them and they turned round in surprise to see the Pied Piper. He twirled his flute and pressed the magical instrument to his lips . . .

"Listen, I don't know who you are or how you know about my curse, but if any of these ogres find out that I'm a—" stammered Fiona.

"A beautiful princess?" replied Shrek.

"You don't know anything about me."

"I know that you sing so beautifully that birds explode," offered Shrek.

"Big deal."

"I know that when you sign your name, you put a heart over the 'i'."

"So what?"

"I know that you don't like the covers wrapped around your feet, and I know that you sleep by candlelight because every time you close your eyes, you're afraid that you're going to wake up back in that tower."

Fiona softened, realizing that maybe Shrek did know her after all.

"But most importantly, Fiona," he continued, "I know that the reason that you turn human every day is because you've never been kissed, well, by me."

As Fiona looked into Shrek's eyes, the Pied Piper's music reached them.

Fiona swung her arms around Shrek's neck, and he wrapped his arms around her waist as she dipped him in an embrace.

"You move fast," murmured Shrek, surprised.

"It's not me doing the moving!"

Shrek and Fiona popped into a tango position and began to dance. Under the control of the Pied Piper, they danced straight towards him.

"Why is this happening?" shouted Fiona.

"Love?" asked Shrek.

"No, I'm being forced to dance! I can't control myself!"

They danced towards the rest of the ogre army, all of them moving and dancing together. The Pied Piper directed them in a conga line straight for Rumpel's palace.

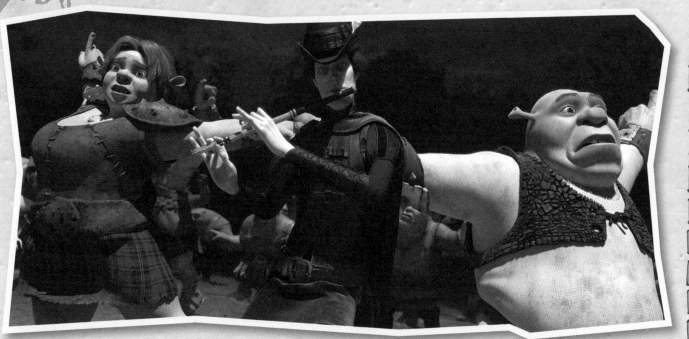

Donkey and Puss arrived to see their friends heading for certain doom.

"We must do something before they fandango themselves into oblivion," said Puss.

"What can we do?" asked Donkey.

"First, you must stop dancing."

"When somebody tooties that flutey, I've got to shake my booty!" Donkey cried.

"Then it is up to me," announced the tubby feline, and he reached out, spread his claws, and scratched Donkey on his hindquarters!

Getting the fright of his life, Donkey reared up on his back legs and took off with Puss (and a rickshaw!) down the hill towards the Pied Piper. Galloping straight for the ogres, he scooped up Fiona and Shrek and sped away from the music.

But the ogre army were not so lucky. Entranced by the music, they were taken to Rumpel's palace and imprisoned in chains. Furious that Shrek and

Fiona had escaped his grasp, Rumpel called to Wolfie, his chief wig-maker.

"Wolfie! My speech wig," he yelled. "Baba! Ready my make-up. And Pied Piper . . . you're fired!"

JOKES

What do you give an ogre
with great big feet?

Lots of space.

Where do Shrek
and Fiona live?

*Ogre the hill
in the swamp!*

What did Shrek say when
someone said he smelt like roses?

"I do snot."

Why did Wolfie laugh so much?

*Because the Three Little Pigs
were hamming it up.*

Why does Shrek have
big nostrils?

*Because he has big
fingers to pick them!*

What did Puss In Boots say
to Rumpel's witches?

Don't try and puss me around!

PICKING
OUT YOUR
DEODORANT

BY
I.M. SMELLY

PICKING OUT YOUR DEODORANT

OGRES AND
OTHER LARGE
THINGS

BY
HUGH MUNGOUS

OGRES AND OTHER LARGE THINGS

What did
Pinocchio say
when someone accused him
of telling a fib?

"I wooden do that!"

DANCE PARTNER

As soon as the Pied Piper starts playing, the ogres start tangoing! Can you draw a line between the matching dancing-ogre silhouettes and work out which lonely ogre doesn't have a dancing partner?

Answers on page 61

Answer

42

CODEBREAKER

Rumpel's a very secretive kind of tyrant. He's written the first draft of his speech in code. Using the key below, can you work out what the wee meany is going to say?

WHOEVER BRINGS ME THIS OGRE SHALL RECEIVE THE . . .

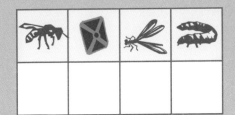

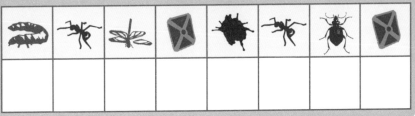

Answers on page 61

The search for Shrek

On the streets of Far Far Away, a light suddenly shone from behind a broken window. The Magic Mirror came to life...

"Attention, citizens! Please stay tuned for a message from our tyrannical dictator!" a voice announced.

"Hello, people," broadcasted Rumpel from the mirror. "It is I, Rumpelstiltskin, shepherd of your dreams. It has been my pleasure to serve you, my loyal subjects, with top-notch service, affection and protection. But recently, a certain somebody has jeopardized our joyous lives. And that somebody is the rat-munching ogre called Shrek!"

And with that, Fiona and Shrek's pictures popped onto the screen around Rumpel.

"Whoever brings me this ogre shall receive... the deal of a lifetime!" offered Rumpel. "All your greatest wishes... Your wildest

dreams... Anything you could ever want. No strings attached! But hurry, this is a limited time offer. So light your torches, sharpen your pitchforks and get your mob on!"

Determined to capture Shrek and claim Rumpel's reward, a crowd of angry villagers marched across Far Far Away to find the wanted ogre.

Behind the ruins of the Poison Apple hid Puss, Donkey and Shrek.

"Look, Shrek," said Donkey, "I know things might look bleak right now, but things will turn out all right in the end. Why, I bet by this time tomorrow—"

"Hey! Don't you understand?" cried Shrek. "There is no tomorrow! There's no day after that and after that! My life was perfect and I'm never going to get it back."

Confused, Donkey asked, "If your life was so perfect, then why did you sign it all away to Rumpelstiltskin in the first place?"

"Because I didn't know what I had until it was gone! All right?!" Shrek answered.

A weird, muffled thumping sound followed by high-pitched grunts filled the silence. Donkey, Shrek and Puss looked down to see . . .

"I'm taking you in!" shouted Gingy as he attacked Shrek's foot with very little result. "Don't try to fight it, ogre . . . The reward is mine!" the cookie warned.

Shrek picked up Gingy.

"Unhand me, green devil!" yelled Gingy. "I'm collecting my bounty! Rumpelstiltskin promised the Deal of a Lifetime for whoever could bring you in!"

"Deal of a Lifetime?" repeated Shrek. "I can still fix this."

Shrek placed Gingy on the ground and told Puss and Donkey to wait for him: this was something he had to sort out on his own.

"OK, Gingy, now tell me about this deal . . ." said Shrek, finally realizing that if he couldn't get his old life back he'd do the next best thing and help Fiona in this one.

But Gingy wasn't there – and Puss seemed to have gingerbread crumbs all around his mouth!

"Oh, were you going to eat that?" he asked.

Inside Rumpel's throne room, the hall was filled with people hoping to cash in on their Deal of a Lifetime by presenting their own fake Shreks.

"Not Shrek! That is not Shrek! Also not Shrek! That is not an ogre, it is a troll. Nice try!" yelled an angry Rumpel as he stomped down the line of hopefuls eager for the reward.

"And what is that supposed to be?" he asked, arriving at Pinocchio, who had painted his dad, Geppetto, green.

"I'm just a frightened old man," whimpered Geppetto.

"Don't listen, these ogres are crafty," answered Pinocchio.

"This is your father painted green," said Rumpel.

"No, it's Shrek. Honest," fibbed Pinocchio, and with that, his nose grew so long it poked Rumpel in the eye.

"Ah!" cried Rumpel. "Can no one bring me Shrek?!"

"Stiltskin!" shouted a voice from the doorway. Rumpel looked over to see Shrek standing there. "I hear you're looking for me."

Thrilled, Rumpel ran over to Shrek.

Shrek plucked a feather from Fifi and prepared to sign the contract. "If I'm turning myself in, I get the Deal of a Lifetime."

"Go ahead and sign it," laughed Rumpel. "Because if you thought you were just going to do-dah-do-dah-do in here and get your life back, uh-uh. Ain't going to happen. Only True Love's Kiss can break your contract."

"I'm not here to get my life back," Shrek replied.

"Then what is it that you want?" asked a very confused Rumpel...

Meanwhile, as Donkey and Puss waited outside the palace, all the ogres that Rumpelstiltskin had captured tumbled out of the sky and crashed to the ground.

"We're free? We're free!" they shouted.

Donkey looked around for his friend but couldn't see him. "Where's Shrek?" he asked.

"This is not good," answered Puss.

"I've got to say, Shrek, that was some pretty heroic stuff," laughed Rumpel as he led Shrek to the dungeon. "Using your Deal of a Lifetime to free all those filthy ogres. I should thank you for making my job so much easier."

"Except I didn't do it for you. I did it for Fiona," replied Shrek.

"I bet she'd be really touched," said Rumpel. "But hey, I guess you can tell her that yourself."

Rumpel stood aside to reveal Fiona chained up on the other side of the room. Shrek was furious.

"Rumpel, we had a deal! You agreed to free all ogres!" he yelled.

"Oh yeah, but Fiona isn't 'all ogre', is she?" grinned Rumpel. "Nobody's smart but me!" he laughed as he left Shrek and Fiona alone.

Inside Rumpel's throne room, his new disco ball was getting hoisted into place.

"My new pretty ball!" exclaimed Rumpel. "Witches! Finally, the moment we've all been waiting for! The main event of the evening!"

The dance floor opened to reveal Shrek and Fiona held captive in the dungeon.

"But now for the real entertainment," shouted Rumpel. "I give you a princess's worst nightmare, Fiona's old flame, the keeper of the Keep . . . Dragon!"

From behind a cloud of smoke Dragon emerged, stalking towards Shrek and Fiona. She reared up, preparing to unleash her fire breath, when . . . someone started to sing! Donkey was standing on top of the disco ball. Puss slid down to join him – and he was wearing his boots!

From inside the ball, came a *toot, toot* as the ogres sounded their battle ear-trumpets. The ball began to rumble and . . . BLAM! . . . the giant disco ball exploded across the dance floor, and the entire ogre army appeared from inside! As the ogres and the witches began to fight, Rumpel was rescued by a witch on her broom.

WHO'S WHO?

Some of the fairytale creatures have disguised themselves as Shrek to claim Rumpel's prize. Can you work out who and find them in the crowd below?

Answers on page 61

Answer:

have disguised themselves as Shrek

DOT-TO-DOT

Use your pencil to join the dots and
discover who has been tempted by
Rumpel's Deal of a Lifetime.

The final countdown

Dragon advanced on Shrek and Fiona as Puss and Donkey rushed to help!

"Donkey! Woo her!" shouted Shrek.

Terrified, Donkey stared into Dragon's eyes, moving in closer, close enough to kiss her, when— "Uh-oh," whimpered Donkey as Dragon revealed her razor-sharp teeth and promptly swallowed Donkey!

Jumping into action, Puss leapt onto Dragon and stabbed his sword into her tail.

"Woo-hoo!" shouted Donkey as Dragon ejected him from her mouth ... and threw him straight onto Baba's broom! "Road trip!" Donkey cried.

Dragon unleashed a huge blast of fire at Fiona and Puss, but when the smoke cleared, they were nowhere to be seen.

Quickly, Shrek and Fiona swung up to the empty ogre cages hanging from the ceiling as Puss climbed to the dance floor above.

* * *

In the throne room, the witches continued to throw pumpkin bombs and skull shackles at the attacking ogres. But as the witches fought back from their brooms, they were suddenly hit by mysterious objects from the battle below.

It was Cookie, flinging her chimichangas!

"Get them while they're hot," she yelled, knocking Baba off her broom and leaving Donkey flying solo!

Shrek and Fiona shared a look of unspoken understanding as Dragon prepared to charge at them. They jumped from the cage and swung around Dragon on their chains, working together to trap her.

"The dragon goes under the bridge . . ." said Shrek, running to the left.

" . . . through the loop . . ." said Fiona, running right.

" . . . and finally . . ." added Shrek.

" . . . into the castle!" they shouted together as they tied up Dragon with a final tug.

Meanwhile, Rumpel was surrounded by ogres. They were coming for him on all sides, attacking the witches with water-filled frogs. But just as they were about to close in on him, Rumpel jumped off the balcony.

"So long! Ha ha!" he shouted as Fifi caught him and flew out of the ogres' reach. As they flew upwards, a skull shackle grabbed Fifi's leg. Shrek had shackled her and was holding tightly to the other end of the chain.

"Come on, Fifi! Flap your wings!" yelled Rumpel frantically.

Shrek grabbed Fiona by the waist as Fifi flew to the window.

"Come on for Daddy! Come on, Fifi!" shouted Rumpel.

With a strong yank, Shrek pulled on the chain attached to Fifi, and the giant bird flailed wildly in the air.

"Fifi, no!" cried Rumpel as he tumbled from Fifi's back, and into . . . Fiona's arms!

"Victory is ours!" shouted Fiona as she threw Rumpel to Brogan. The other ogres gathered around their prize.

"Cookie, it looks like we're having curly-toed weirdo for breakfast," smiled Brogan.

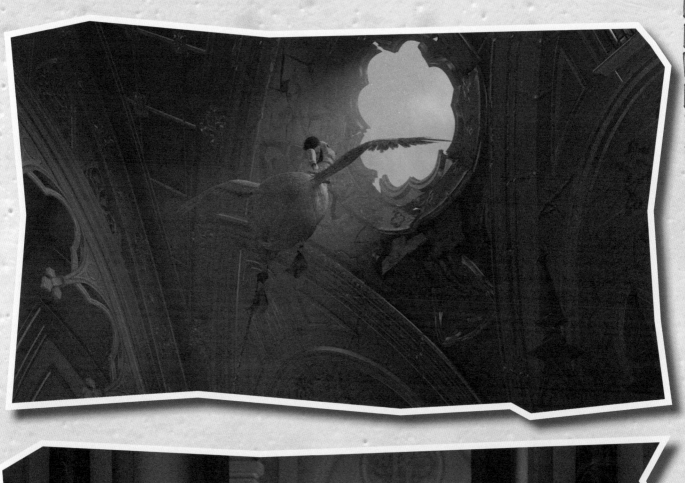

As the ogres celebrated their victory, Shrek and Fiona shared a moment.

"Hey, we make a pretty good team," she said.

"You have no idea," Shrek replied.

The two ogres smiled at each other tenderly as the first rays of morning sunlight trickled into the palace. Shrek followed Fiona's gaze. As he looked down, he saw his fingers slowly beginning to fade from existence.

Fiona rushed to Shrek's side; his body had started disappearing too.

"His day is up!" laughed Rumpel. "His day is—" The ogre holding Rumpel in a headlock squeezed Rumpel's neck, cutting him off.

Puss respectfully removed his hat as Fiona cradled Shrek's head.

"There has to be something we can do," said Fiona desperately.

"You've already done everything for me, Fiona. You gave me a home and a family," smiled Shrek warmly.

"You have kids?" she asked.

"We have kids. Fergus, Farkle, and a little girl named . . ."

". . . Felicia," she guessed. "I've always wanted to have a daughter named Felicia."

Shrek reached into his vest and pulled out Felicia's Sir Squeakles toy.

"And someday you will," he whispered. "The best part of my day, Fiona, was falling in love with you all over again."

As the last of Shrek began to fade away, Fiona

leaned in and gently kissed him on the lips. Then Shrek was gone. The last drop of sand fell in the hourglass. But something strange had happened. As the clouds parted and the morning sunlight shone, Puss noticed that Fiona hadn't changed into her human form.

"Fiona . . . you are still . . . an ogre," he said.

Fiona looked at her ogre hands in disbelief.

"True Love's form," she said.

"Impossible!" shouted Rumpel.

As Fiona realized that Shrek was her True Love, the winds picked up and began swirling around them. Ogres and witches suddenly began to tear apart, Fifi disappeared, and everything around Rumpel vanished in a flurry of magical chaos until everything went black . . .

Home Sweet Home

He stared dumbfounded at his surroundings – his family and friends were right back where he had left them. When he saw Fiona, he threw his arms joyously around her.

"Shrek, are you OK?" she asked.

"I've never been better," he grinned.

Shrek heard his ogre babies practise roaring just like their dad, and he hugged them all, one by one.

Shrek looked into Fiona's eyes and said: "You know, I always thought I rescued you from the Dragon's Keep."

"You did," answered Fiona.

"ROOOOOOOAAAAAAARRRR!"

Shrek's eyes snapped open and he found himself back in the Candy Apple surrounded by a happy crowd cheering him on for his awesome roar.

"No, it was you who rescued me," he told her.

The crowd cheered once more as Shrek took Fiona in his arms and kissed her, and they all lived Happily Ever After.

SHREK TRIVIA

Take this ogre-ific quiz to find out how much
you know about Shrek and his friends!

1. Shrek has three ogre babies called . . .

a. Fergus, Farkle and Fergle

b. Farkle, Felicia and Fergus

c. Fergie, Furgie and Fargus

2. Shrek's daughter has a toy called . . .

a. Sir Squeakles

b. Miss Teddy

c. Shrek Junior

3. Who asked Shrek for a big roar at the Candy Apple?

a. Rumpelstiltskin

b. Fiona

c. Butter Pants

4. Shrek signed a contract that made him . . .

a. An ogre for a day

b. A prince for a week

c. A toad for a year

5. Who helped Shrek work out the exit clause of the contract?

a. Fiona

b. Puss In Boots

c. Donkey

Answers
on page 61

6. To break the contract, he needed . . .

a. To become an ogre warrior

b. True Love's Kiss

c. Try Lou's Bliss

7. What food led Donkey and Shrek to the ogre camp?

a. Doughnuts

b. Pizza

c. Waffles

8. Rumpel's beloved pet goose is called . . .

a. Fifi

b. Didi

c. Honker

9. Why doesn't Rumpel free Fiona after Shrek turns himself in to save all ogres?

a. Because Rumpel loves her

b. Because Fiona's not "all ogre"

c. Because Shrek didn't want to save Fiona again

10. What happens to Shrek at the end of his day?

a. He disappears for ever

b. He gets eaten by Dragon

c. He ends up right back where he started

Answers on page 61

ACTIVITY ANSWERS

Page 13:

 24   15   18

Page 18: C

Page 21: 32

Page 24:

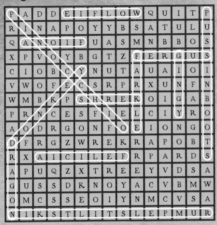

Page 25:

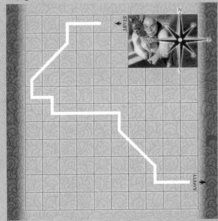

Page 26: TRUE LOVE'S KISS

Pages 32–33:

Page 34:

Page 35:

Page 42: D

Page 43:
DEAL OF A LIFETIME

Page 50: Blind Mouse, Gingy,
Pinnochio, Butter Pants

Pages 59-60:
1–b, 2–a, 3–c, 4–a, 5–c, 6–b, 7–c,
8–a, 9–b, 10–c